Everyone Loves Fox + Chick!

A Theodor Seuss Geisel Honor Book

A New York Times Notable Children's Book

An NPR Best Book of the Year

A Publishers Weekly Best Book of the Year

A School Library Journal Best Book of the Year

An ALA Notable Children's Book

A Boston Globe Best Book of the Year

Also Available!

To Robin Smith -S. R.

First Chronicle Books LLC paperback edition, published in 2020.

Originally published in hardcover in 2018 by Chronicle Books LLC.

ISBN 978-1-4521-8077-9

The Library of Congress has cataloged the original edition as follows:

Library of Congress Cataloging-in-Publication Data

Names: Ruzzier, Sergio, 1966- author, illustrator.

Title: The party and other stories / by Sergio Ruzzier.

Description: San Francisco, California : Chronicle Books LLC, 2018

Series: Fox Chick ; book 1 Summary: Fox and Chick are unlikely friends, but somehow they seem to get along together, even though Fox is calm and thoughtful, and Chick has is hyperactive and flighty.

Identifiers: LCCN 2017046551 ISBN 9781452152882 alk. paper

Subjects: LCSH: Foxes -Juvenile fiction. Chicks-Juvenile fiction. Friendship-Juvenile fiction. Humorous stories. CYAC: Foxes-Fiction. Chickens-Fiction. Friendship-Fiction. Humorous stories. LCGFT: Humorous fiction.

Classification: LCC PZ7.R9475 Par 2018 DDC E-dc23 LC record available at https://lccn.loc.gov/2017046551

Manufactured in China.

Book design by Sara Gillingham Studio.

Paperback design by Riza Cruz.

Handlettering by Sergio Ruzzier.

The illustrations in this book were rendered in pen, ink, and watercolor.

10 9 8 7 6 5 4 3 2

Chronicle Books LLC
680 Second Street
San Francisco, California 94107
www.chroniclekids.com

SERGIO RUZZIER'S

FOX + CHICK

THE PARTY

and Other Stories

chronicle books · san francisco

CONTENTS

The Party 2

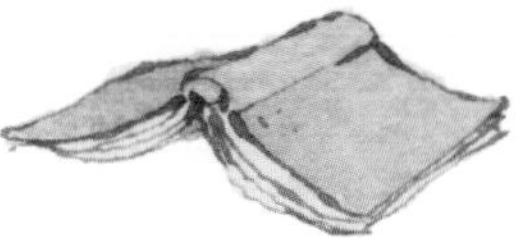

Good Soup 18

Sit Still 32

THE PARTY

KNOCK
KNOCK

It's me:
Chick!

I know it's
you, Chick!
I can
see you!

What
are you
doing?

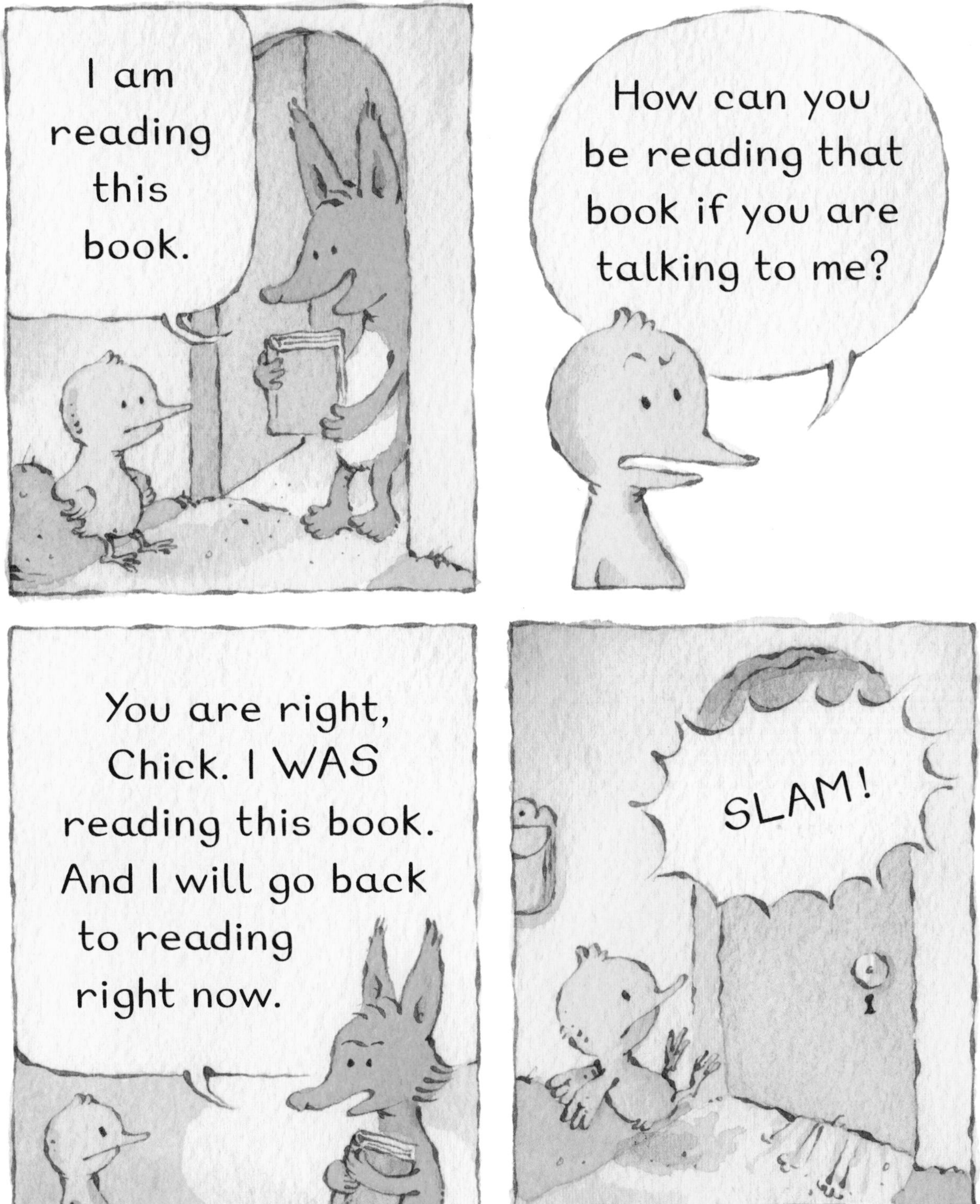

You are right, Chick. I WAS reading this book. And I will go back to reading right now.

It's still me:
Chick!

May I use your
bathroom?

Of course you may.

Thank you, Fox.
Very kind of you.

TICK
TOCK

TICK
TOCK

TICK
TOCK

TICK
TOCK

TICK
TOCK

Chick, are you okay?

CRASH!
THUD!
SPLASH!

Chick, I am coming in!

Chick!

What is going on in here?
Can't you tell? I am having a party with my friends.
In my bathroom?!

Oh, I see . . .
Let's go, guys.

I guess he didn't mean it when he said I could use his bathroom.

GOOD SOUP

Fox, foxes are supposed to eat field mice, not carrots!

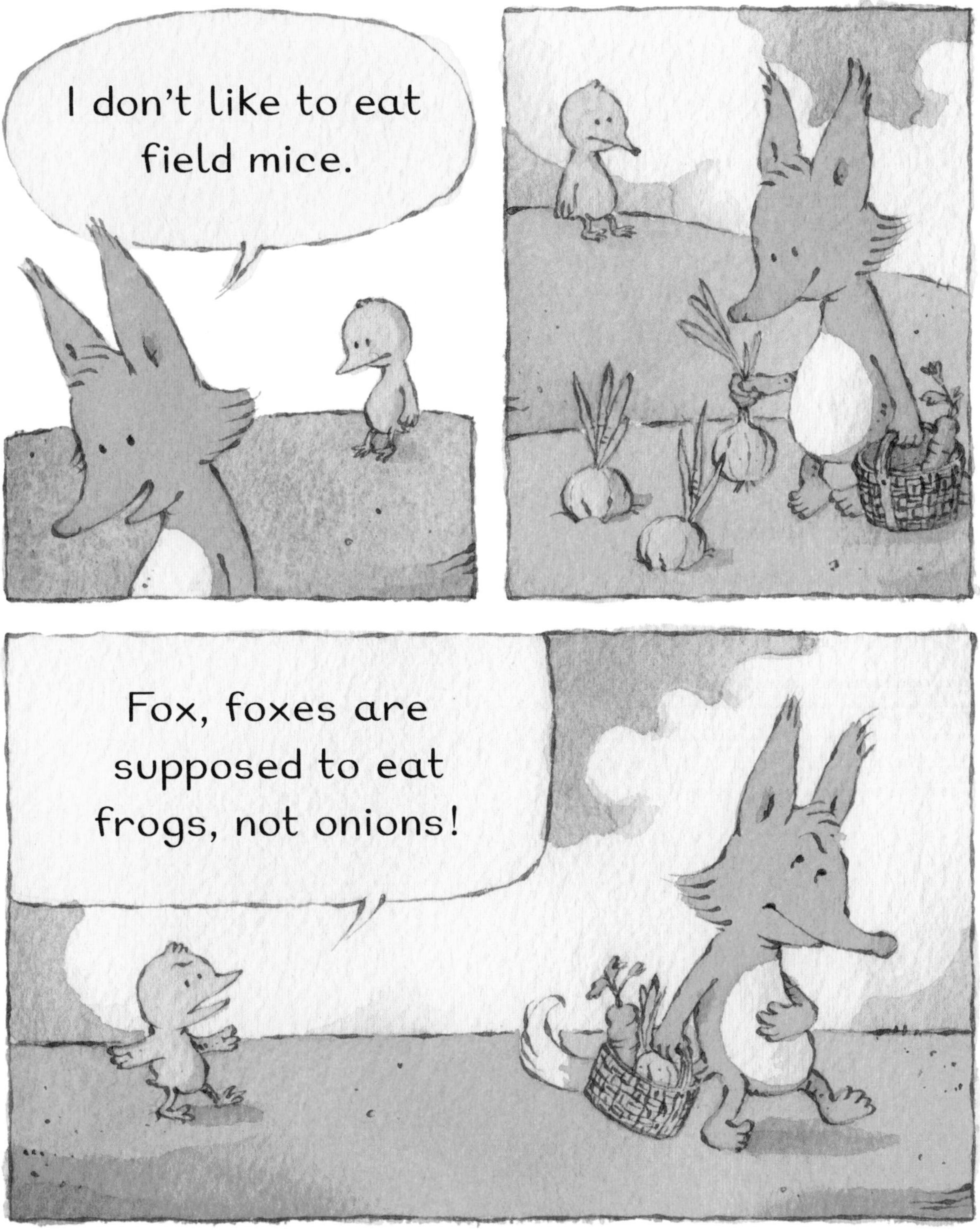

Fox, foxes are supposed to eat frogs, not onions!

Fox, foxes are supposed to eat moles, not potatoes!

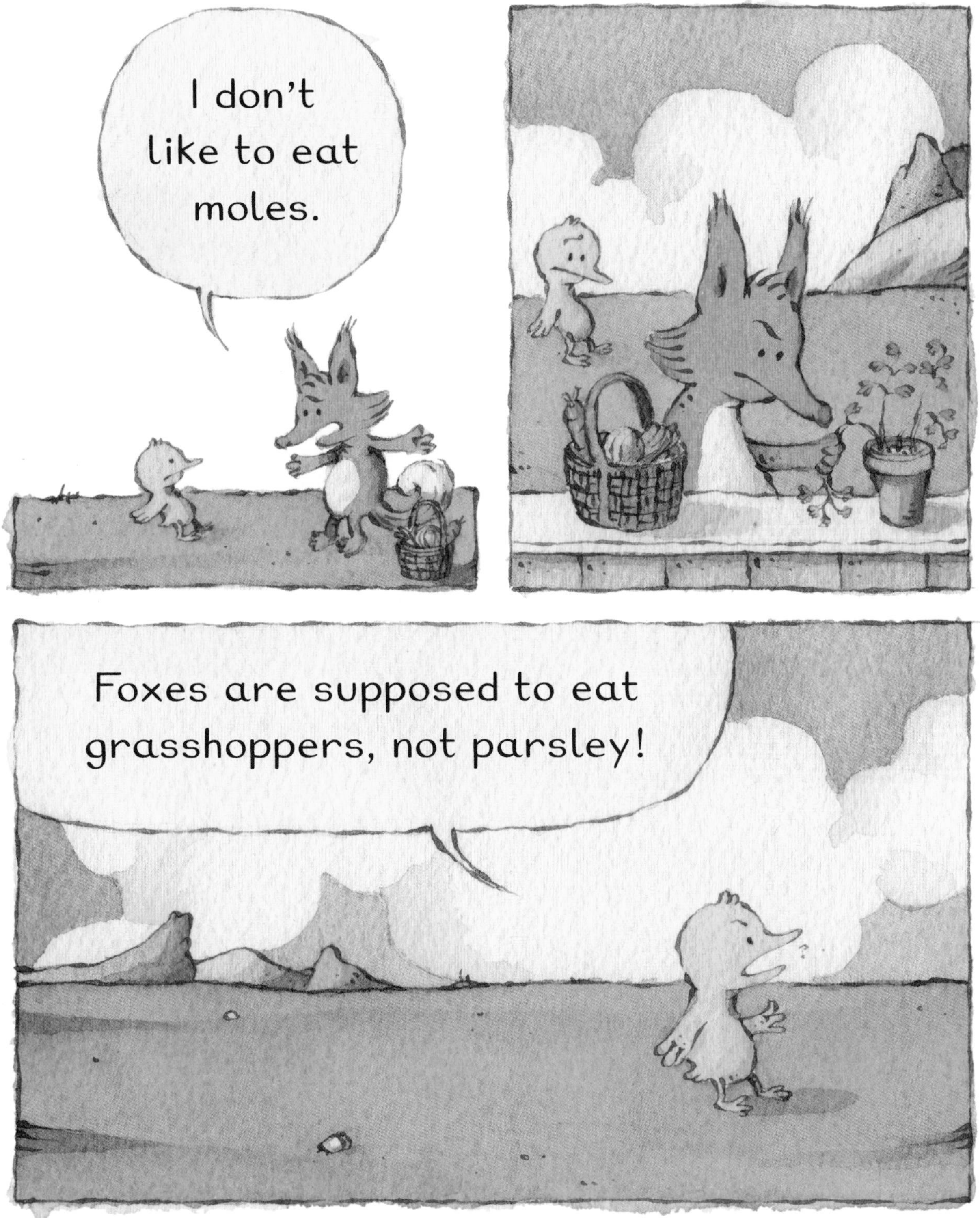

Foxes are supposed to eat grasshoppers, not parsley!

I don't like to eat grasshoppers.

Sometimes I wonder if you are a real fox.

What else do you think foxes are supposed to eat?

Foxes are supposed to eat chipmunks.

And they're supposed to eat squirrels . . .

lizards . . .

and little birds.

Little birds?

Yes, Fox,
little bir . . .

Uh-oh.

AHHHHH!

Chick!

Good soup.

Thank you,
Chick.

I am glad you don't like to eat little birds, Fox.
At least not today.

SIT STILL

This is a good spot.

I will paint a nice landscape.

What are you doing, Fox?
I'm painting a landscape.

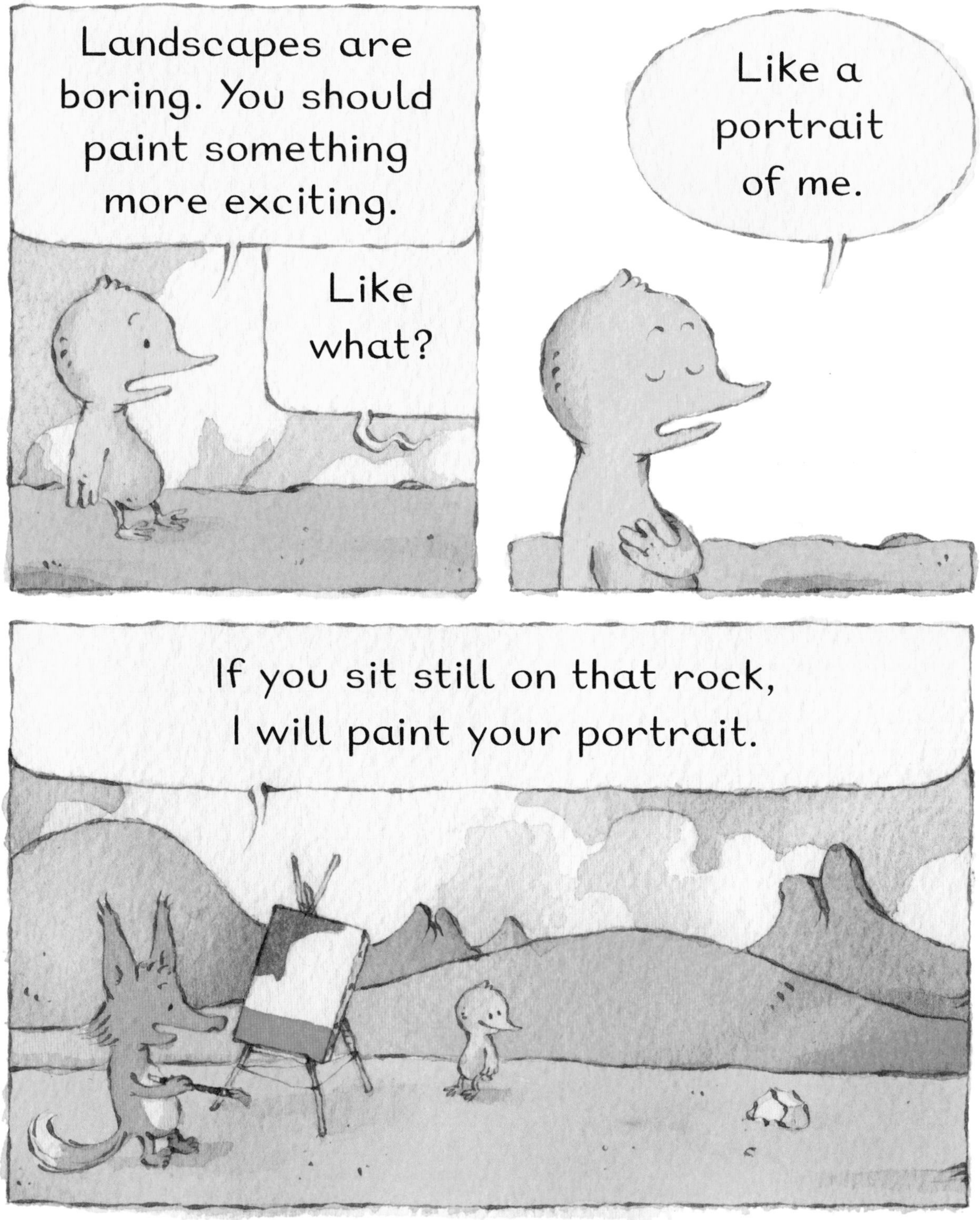

If you sit still on that rock, I will paint your portrait.

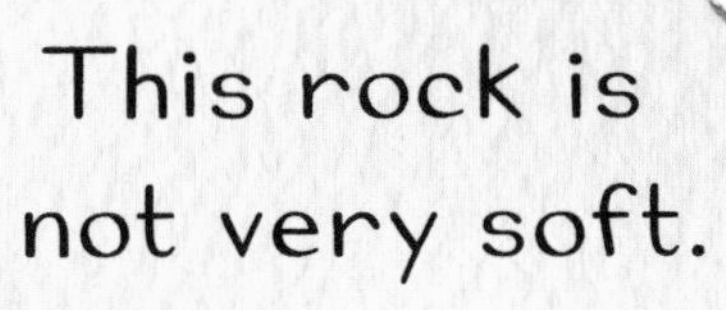

Of course it's not very soft. It is a rock.

I will go and get a pillow. Then I will sit still on that rock.

Fox, you can paint my portrait now.
Just sit still, please.

I am hungry.

You just ate three bowls of soup.

I will go and get a snack. Then I will sit very still on that rock.

CRUNCH

Of course you are thirsty. You ate a whole bag of potato chips.

SLURP

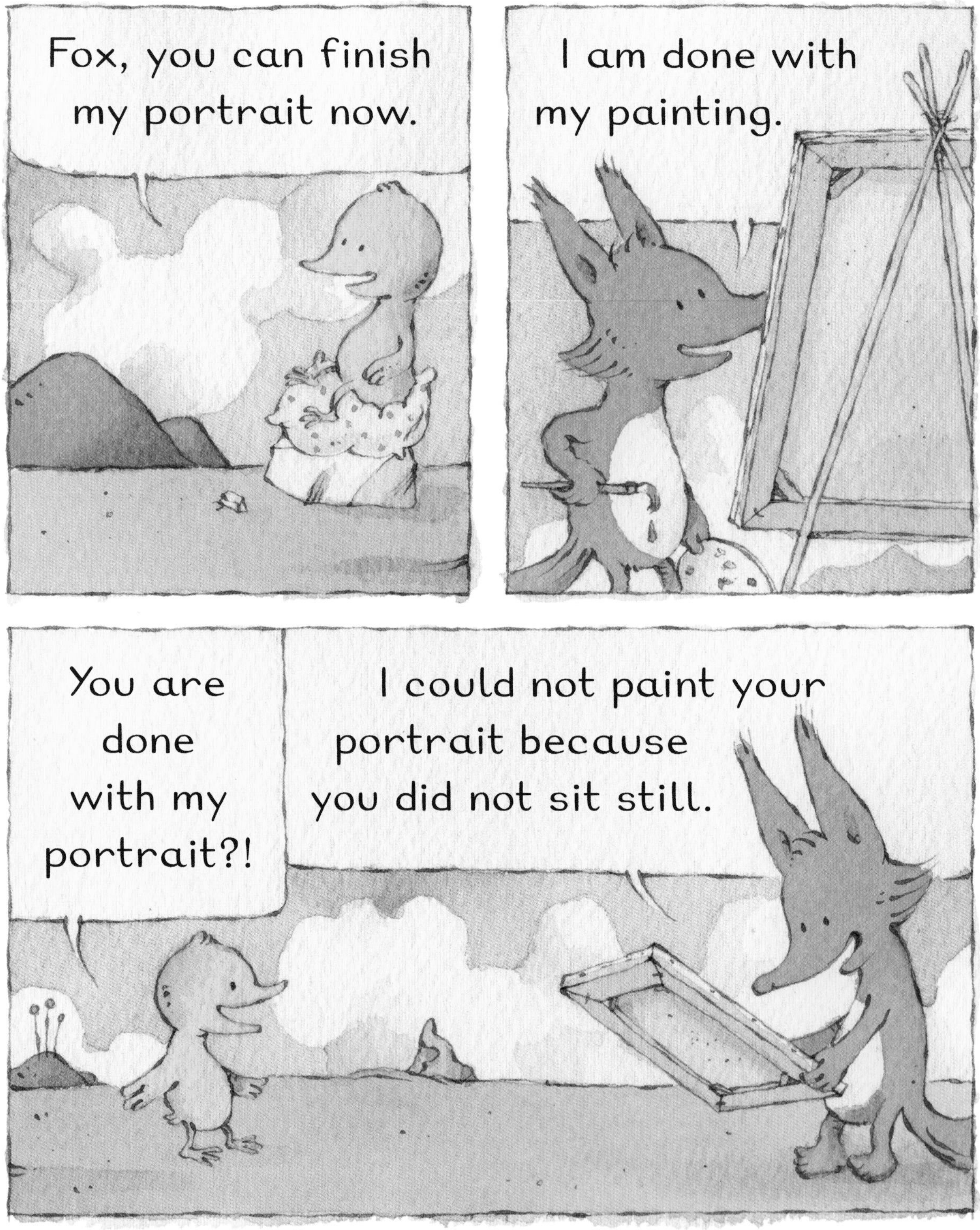

You are
done
with my
portrait?!

I could not paint your
portrait because
you did not sit still.

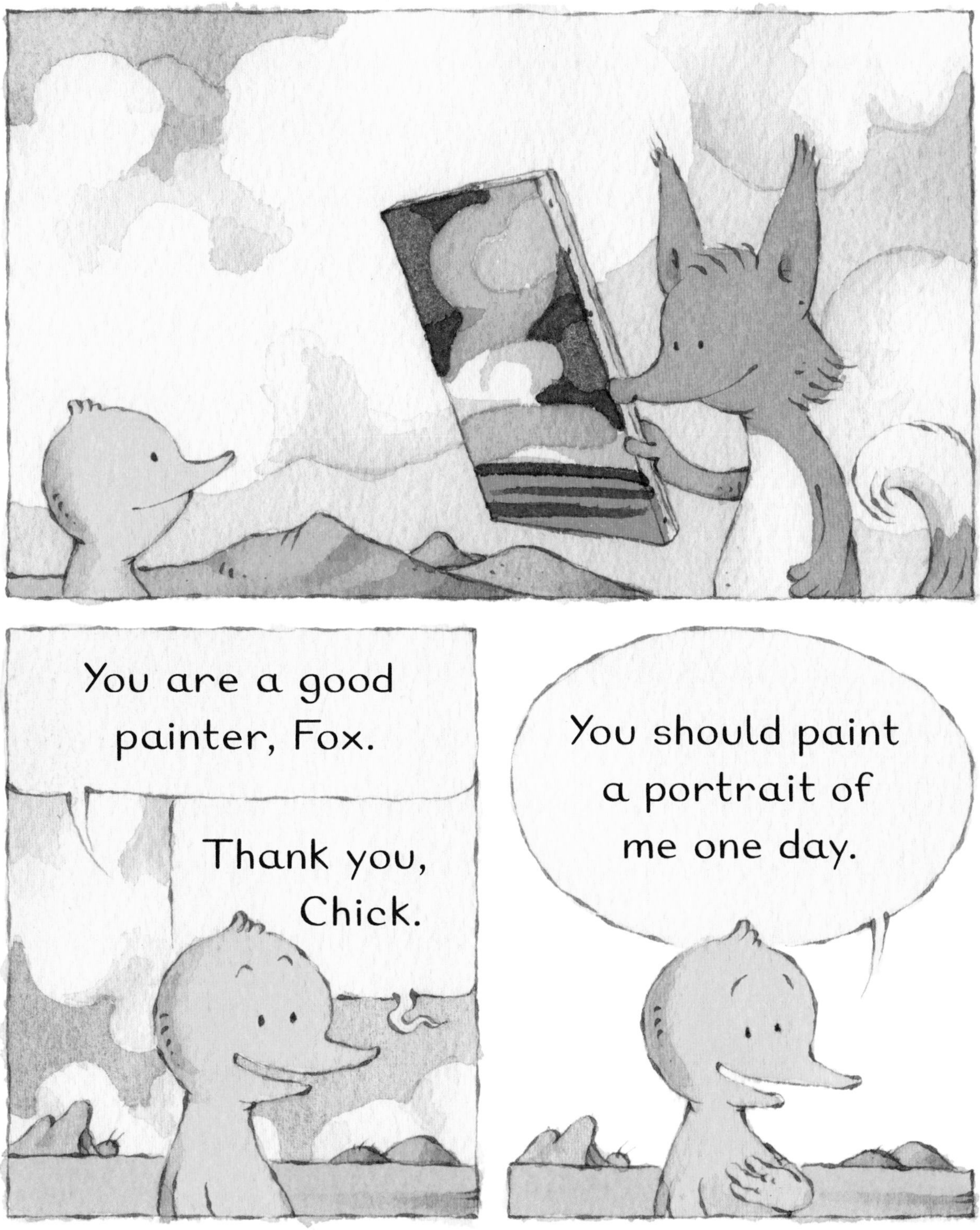

You should paint a portrait of me one day.

Great idea, Chick.
One day I will.

It's the end, Fox!
Only for now, Chick.

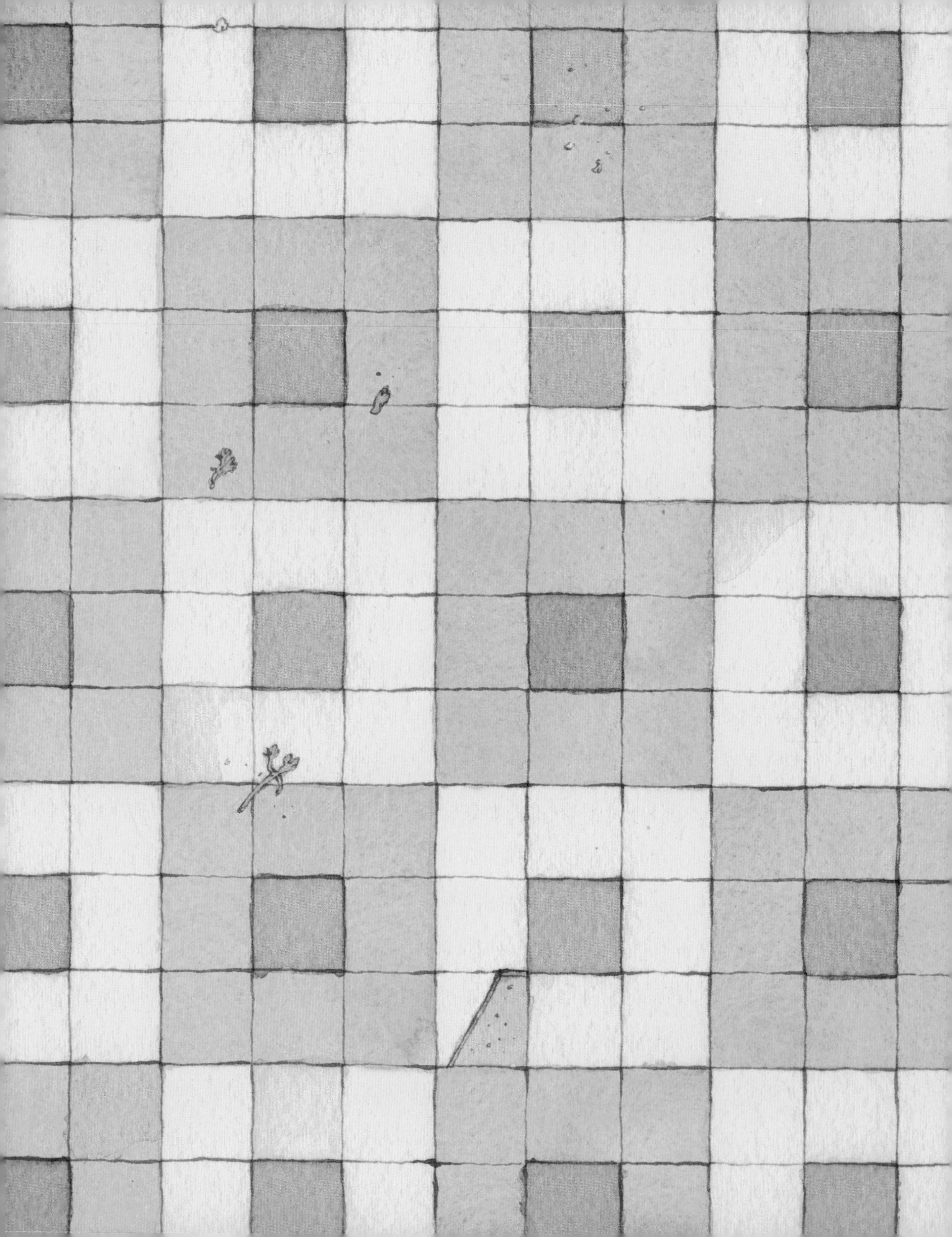

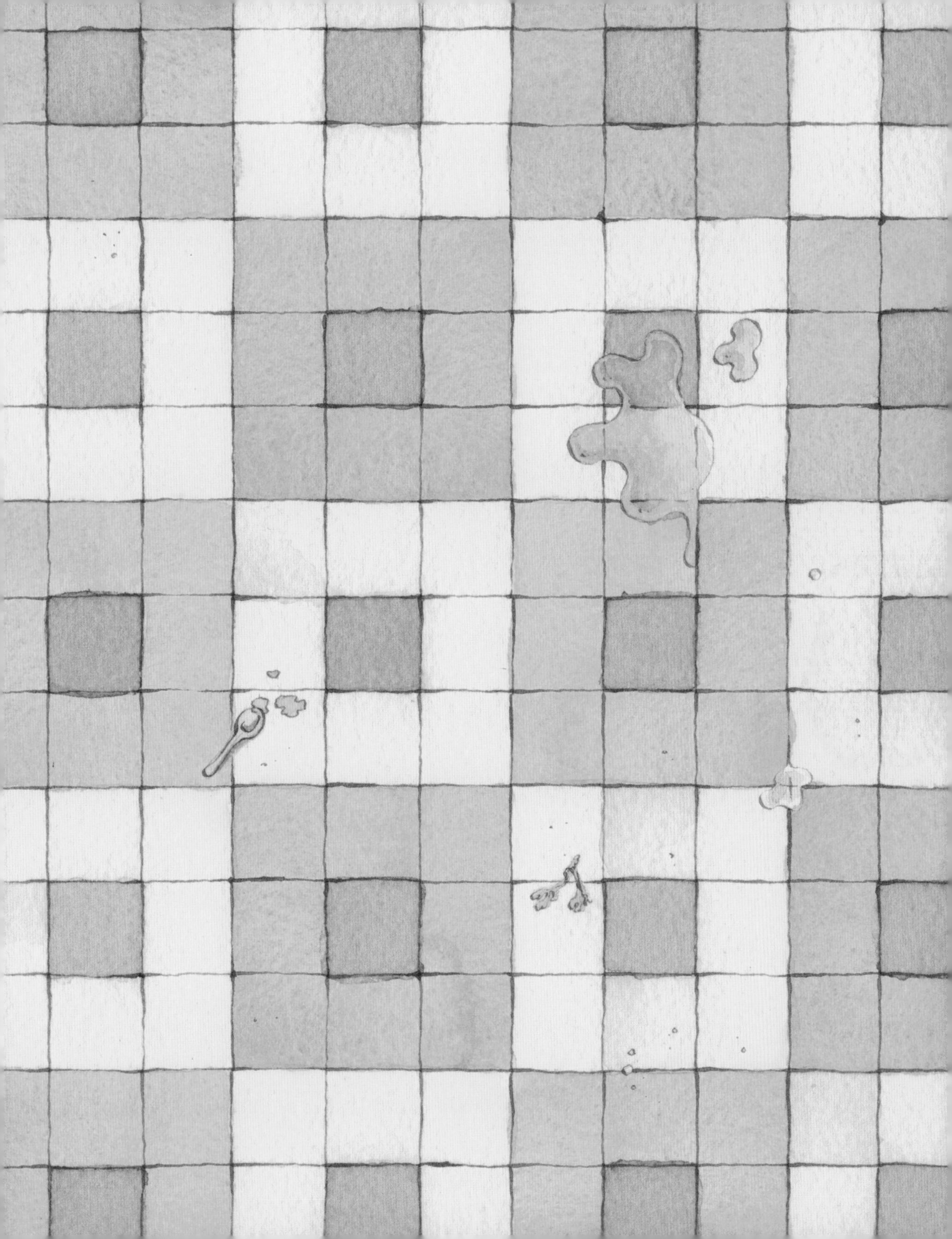

Also by Sergio Ruzzier
This Is Not a Picture Book!

"Sweet, profound. Pays a sneaky tribute to the power of words and pictures."
—*The New York Times*

A New York Times
Notable Children's Book

A School Library Journal
Best Children's Book of the Year

A Publishers Weekly
Best Book of the Year

A Huffington Post
Best Picture Book of the Year
Honorable Mention

A Parents' Choice Gold Award

★ *School Library Journal*,
starred review

★ *Kirkus Reviews*,
starred review

★ *Publishers Weekly*,
starred review

Sergio Ruzzier is a 2011 Sendak Fellow who has written and illustrated many critically acclaimed children's books. Born in Milan, Italy, he now divides his time between Brooklyn, New York, and the Apennine Mountains in Italy.